7

8

9

10

11

12

OTHER BOOKS BY INGRI AND EDGAR PARIN D'AULAIRE

D'Aulaires' Book of Animals

D'Aulaires' Book of Norse Myths

D'Aulaires' Book of Trolls

The Terrible Troll-Bird

The Two Cars

FOXIE
THE SINGING DOG

INGRI and EDGAR PARIN D'AULAIRE

THE NEW YORK REVIEW CHILDREN'S COLLECTION

New York

THIS IS A NEW YORK REVIEW BOOK

PUBLISHED BY THE NEW YORK REVIEW OF BOOKS

1755 Broadway, New York, NY 10019

www.nyrb.com

Published in the United States of America

Library of Congress Cataloging-in-Publication Data

D'Aulaire, Ingri, 1904–1980.
Foxie : the singing dog / by Ingri and Edgar Parin d'Aulaire.
p. cm. — (New York Review Books children's collection)
Summary: A lost dog's luck makes her fat and famous, but when given a chance she proves he still thinks there is no place like home.
ISBN 978-1-59017-264-3 (alk. paper)
[1. Dogs--Fiction.] I. D'Aulaire, Edgar Parin, 1898-1986. II. Title.

PZ10.3.A92Fo5 2007
[Fic]—dc22
2007027028

ISBN 978-1-59017-264-3

Cover design by Louise Fili Ltd.

This book is printed on acid-free paper.

Manufactured in China by P. Chan & Edward, Inc.

1 3 5 7 9 10 8 6 4 2

"Fox-ie!" cried a shrill voice.

The little dog with a head like a fox and a tail like a cinnamon roll woke up with a start.

She had been dreaming happily of soupbones, and when she opened one eye she saw

a real bone right in front of her nose! But as Foxie jumped for it the bone jumped, too. Her master liked to play and tease Foxie, who was always hungry.

"Come and play," said her master. So Foxie chased the bone. She sat on her tail. She stood on her nose. Her eyes begged and her tail wagged, "Please, I am hungry." Her master thought it was fun for a while, but then he thought of something else. He put

the bone into his pocket and skipped off down the street. He forgot all about Foxie, but poor, little hungry Foxie could not forget the bone, so out of her yard she ran.

She trailed her master street up and street down through a forest of feet. Sometimes she lost sight of him, but the smell of the bone led her on. Once, for a moment, she forgot the bone and stopped to make friends with a black poodle that came tripping toward

her. But the beautiful dog was haughty. "Mutt," she sniffed, and sailed on, leaving a scent of juicy roasts. That reminded Foxie of her bone. She sniffed around among people's feet until she had picked up her master's trail again.

But before Foxie had caught up with her master a loud burst of music hit her ears.
A band of musicians came marching down the street, playing as loudly as they could.

Foxie could not bear music. It hurt her in every joint.

She whined and she wailed, she turned round and round, and howled.

"Look at the dog trying to sing," said the people who had stopped to enjoy the music.

Foxie closed her eyes and howled on. When at last she recovered herself the music was gone, and so was her master's trail. For all that she sniffed she could not find it.

She could not find her master and the bone. She could not even find her way home.
It grew dark and it started to rain. Foxie was lost!

She huddled in a doorway, overcome by hunger and grief. At last she fell asleep dreaming hungrily of bones and the lovely smell of juicy roasts that had perfumed the beautiful poodle.

Suddenly the door behind her was flung open. A man stepped on her. "Where do you come from you poor little fox?" asked the man. "You must be lost, and you look hungry. You had better come with me." He reached down to pet her.

Foxie wanted to growl and bite. But the man was fat and friendly looking and smelled so nicely of soup and chops. So she rubbed her head against his hand.

Gently the fat man picked Foxie up and took her home with him. "You would be a nice little dog if you were not so skinny," he said. "Come here and eat. But what is

your name? You look like a hungry little fox. I will call you Foxie." Foxie wagged her
tail in approval and gobbled the delicious food.

She ate and she ate till she almost burst. Then she went to sleep under the fat man's

bed. Toward morning she woke and began to sniff around to find out what kind of house she had come to. When she came to a door she pushed it open and—

WHOOSH, a striped monster with gleaming eyes leaped at her.

A ghostly scream came from a corner.

"Help! murder!" barked Foxie. The fat man came running and turned on the light. And what do you think? The monster was a big, striped tomcat and the screaming ghost was a rooster. "You poor little Foxie! Were you so scared?" The fat man laughed. "But now you must all be friends," he said, and went back to his room.

It came easy to Foxie to be friendly. The rooster was friendly, too. He stepped aside and let Foxie sample his food. It did not taste good, but it was food. But the cat was stingy and had no manners. He closed his eyes and pretended to be asleep, but his claws were out. Foxie did not dare go near his dish.

Then the fat man came back with another bowl. "Plenty of food for all," he said, and gave Foxie a dish of her own. Foxie liked her own food. Still, it would have been fun to know if the cat's meat was better.

"Now for some music," said the fat man. He pulled out a flute and began to play. The cat sat down at a piano and pawed the keys, sometimes hard, sometimes soft, but always with much feeling. The rooster stretched his neck and crowed with all his might. The music went up and down Foxie's spine. She could not stand it, she howled.

"What rare luck," cried the fat man. "A singing dog! I have a trio! Again," he said, "again and again!" And the cat played, the rooster crowed, and Foxie waited till they were all tired out.

"Now we will do some tricks," the fat man said. The rooster played dead. The cat turned somersaults. And the fat man praised them and gave them tidbits from his pockets. When Foxie saw this she stood on her nose. So she had a tidbit, too. The fat man

was pleased. And Foxie knew that every time she could do a new trick she would get a tidbit out of his pocket. She worked hard.

Foxie grew fat and sleek and lovely. All day long she was happy and busy learning new tricks, but when it grew dark the fat man tucked the cat and the rooster under his cloak and went out. Then Foxie thought of her master and was homesick until

she fell asleep and began to dream. As she grew fatter her dreams became fancier.
She no longer dreamed of ordinary bones but of turkey necks and juicy roasts. Sometimes she dreamed of a creature that was half her master and half the black poodle.

It played with her and teased her. They ran merrily side by side and together they sneaked up on the cat and stole his food.

In the morning Foxie tried to do it alone.
But the cat was too smart to be caught napping!

All Foxie could do was to work harder than ever on her tricks to show the fat man that she was really much smarter than the cat. And at last one day he said, "Foxie, now I think you are ready."

He dressed Foxie and the cat and the rooster in fancy clothes, and when it grew dark he stuffed them all inside his cloak and went out.

It was hot and dark inside the cloak and they all struggled and pushed to get on top of one another.

At last the fat man flung open his cloak and said "Hop!" Wherever Foxie looked there were faces. She was bewildered. But when the fat man pulled out his flute, the

cat ran for the piano and the rooster began to crow. Then Foxie sat up on her hind legs and howled louder than ever before. From all sides came a roar of applause.

The fat man bowed. Foxie jumped up on his back. The cat jumped up on Foxie and

the rooster perched himself on top of the cat. Together they made the bow that the fat
man had taught them. It was a tremendous success.

But through the cheering Foxie heard a shrill little voice that called "Foxie." THAT
was a beautiful sound to Foxie's ears. It was the voice of her master, the boy.

With a leap of joy Foxie sent her comrades flying. She dived straight into the sea of

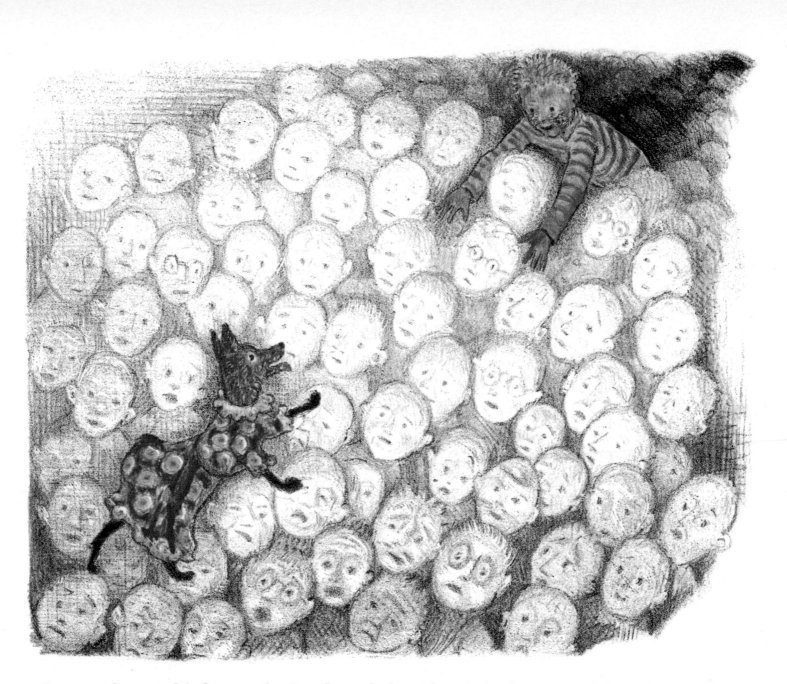

faces and scrambled over the heads and shoulders into the arms of her master.

She forgot the friendly rooster. She forgot the stingy cat. She forgot the kind fat man and all his tidbits. She looked at her master with loving and questioning eyes.

"Oh, Foxie," said her master, "I'll promise never to tease you again!" Foxie wagged her tail in approval. But what she really wanted to ask was where he had hidden the soupbone he had in his pocket the day she was lost.

INGRI MORTENSON and EDGAR PARIN D'AULAIRE met at art school in Munich in 1921. Edgar's father was a noted Italian portrait painter, his mother a Parisian. Ingri, the youngest of five children, traced her lineage back to the Viking kings.

The couple married in Norway, then moved to Paris. As Bohemian artists, they often talked about emigrating to America. "The enormous continent with all its possibilities and grandeur caught our imagination," Edgar later recalled.

A small payment from a bus accident provided the means. Edgar sailed alone to New York where he earned enough by illustrating books to buy passage for his wife. Once there, Ingri painted portraits and hosted modest dinner parties. The head librarian of the New York Public Library's juvenile department attended one of those. Why, she asked, didn't they create picture books for children?

The d'Aulaires published their first children's book in 1931. Next came three books steeped in the Scandinavian folklore of Ingri's childhood. Then the couple turned their talents to the history of their new country. The result was a series of beautifully illustrated books about American heroes, one of which, *Abraham Lincoln*, won the d'Aulaires the American Library Association's Caldecott Medal. Finally they turned to the realm of myths.

The d'Aulaires worked as a team on both art and text throughout their joint career. Originally, they used stone lithography for their illustrations. A single four-color illustration required four slabs of Bavarian limestone that weighed up to two hundred pounds apiece. The technique gave their illustrations an uncanny hand-drawn vibrancy. When, in the early 1960s, this process became too expensive, the d'Aulaires switched to acetate sheets which closely approximated the texture of lithographic stone.

In their nearly five-decade career, the d'Aulaires received high critical acclaim for their distinguished contributions to children's literature. They were working on a new book when Ingri died in 1980 at the age of seventy-five. Edgar continued working until he died in 1985 at the age of eighty-six.

13

14

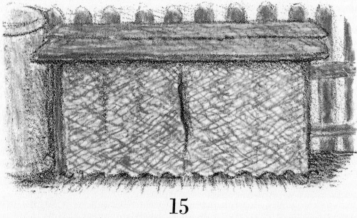

15

16

17

18